W9-BHY-994

For Jim and Lee and Megan and Juren,
who were there when it happened
S. P.

To all my nieces and nephews
J. W.

Reprinted by arrangement with Simon & Schuster *Books for Young Readers*, a Division of
Simon & Schuster Inc., for Silver Burdett Ginn Inc.

SIMON AND SCHUSTER BOOKS FOR YOUNG READERS
Simon & Schuster Building, Rockefeller Center, 1230 Avenue of the Americas,
New York, New York 10020. Text copyright © 1990 by Susan Pearson. Illustrations
copyright © 1990 by James Warhola. All rights reserved including the right of
reproduction in whole or in part in any form. SIMON AND SCHUSTER BOOKS FOR
YOUNG READERS is a trademark of Simon & Schuster Inc.
Designed by Lucille Chomowicz
Manufactured in Mexico   10 9 8 7 6 5 4 3 2

Library of Congress Cataloging in Publication Data: Pearson, Susan. Well, I never!
Summary: A topsy-turvy day on the farm results in misplaced breakfast food, flying
pigs, and farm buildings in the clouds.   [1. Humorous stories.   2. Farm life—
Fiction.]   I. Warhola, James, ill.   II. Title. PZ7.P323316We   1990 [Fic]—dc20
ISBN 0-663-56234-1

WELL, I NEVER!

by Susan Pearson
illustrated by James Warhola

INEZ CARROLL ELEMENTARY

SIMON AND SCHUSTER BOOKS FOR YOUNG READERS

Published by Simon & Schuster Inc.
New York • London • Toronto • Sydney • Tokyo • Singapore

It rained so hard
on Friday night the corn
had grown as tall as trees
by morning. Mavis got
lost in it when she went
for the mail, and we
didn't see her again
till dinnertime.

Then Sidney forgot to shut the cage door and his mice got out. They ran straight to the kitchen, where Aunt Bertha was fixing breakfast. She jumped right up on the counter top and turned as white as a sheet. Then her hair turned white, too. After that, all she could cook was white food.

Uncle Fred made pancakes for us then, but he burned them. He fed them to the goats instead, which would have been all right except for the syrup. The goats got it all over themselves. After that they stuck to everything.

Pa went off to bale the hay, but he must have been woolgathering, 'cause he baled the sheep instead.

Ma fed popcorn to the chickens by mistake, and it popped inside their stomachs. They spent the next hour and a half bouncing on and off the barn roof with Ma running back and forth beneath them trying to catch their eggs in the laundry basket.

Grandma was so busy watching Ma and laughing that she poured a box of laundry soap into the pig slops. The pigs ate it anyway. Then they started blowing bubbles. Then they lifted right up off the ground. Sidney and I caught them with our butterfly nets and tied them to the fence so they wouldn't blow away.

The horses were so surprised to see pigs flying around that their tails all curled, but Grandma ironed them straight again in the laundry room.

The cows forgot the way to the pasture and got tangled in the laundry. They finally got loose and wandered off. Sidney and I found them in the melon patch dressed in Ma's nightie and Aunt Bertha's girdle and Grandpa's Valentine boxer shorts.

When we got back to the barnyard, Pa was sitting on top
of the barn. So was the tractor.

Someone left the checkerboard leaning on its side in the closet, and when Grandpa and I found it, all the black squares had fallen to the bottom. Grandma made us a new board in the waffle iron, but the squares were so small we had to play with peas, which made it hard to get kinged. The peas kept rolling off and getting lost.

Ma got out the vacuum to clean them up, but her mind just wasn't on it, and before she knew it she'd vacuumed up every one of Eleanor's Lincoln Logs, all six of Fritzi's puppies, and Pa's favorite chair.

"Oh, dear," she said. "We've certainly all had our heads in the clouds this morning."

"You can say that again," said Sidney, pointing out the window. We looked through the lace curtains at a cloud floating by.

"Well, I never!" said Aunt Bertha, and we all ran outside to see what was up.

We were. The end of our road didn't meet up with State Highway 32 anymore; it met up with sky. State Highway 32 was about three thousand feet below us—we could just make it out between the clouds.

Ma grabbed her kerchief as a plane whizzed by right in front of us.

"Gracious," she said, "I hope Mavis hasn't fallen off."

Just then Delmore drove up in the pickup truck. Mavis was with him. He'd found her wandering through the corn singing, "Show me the way to go home."

"Well, that's a relief," said Ma. "Now all we have to do is figure out a way to get down from here."

"Simple," said Sidney. "Just tie something heavy to a rope and drop it down. It'll pull us after it."

So Delmore ran to find a rope. He tied one end of it around the barn, and Sidney tied the other end to the pickup. Then we lowered the pickup. The farm dropped about a thousand feet, then stopped.

"We need more weight," called Sidney. So Delmore brought the horses. Sidney tied them onto the rope and lowered them, and we dropped another five hundred feet.

Delmore brought the sofa next, then the piano, and finally the cows. That did it. We were back in Iowa.

Grandma sewed us down with fishing line, and everything went back to normal. Fritzi's puppies popped out of the vacuum cleaner, the black squares on the checkerboard moved back up to where they belonged, the corn shrank, and the pigs came down to earth.

"I'm certainly glad that's over," said Ma as we sat down to a dinner of white rice, white bread, white potatoes, white onions, white cheese, and milk.

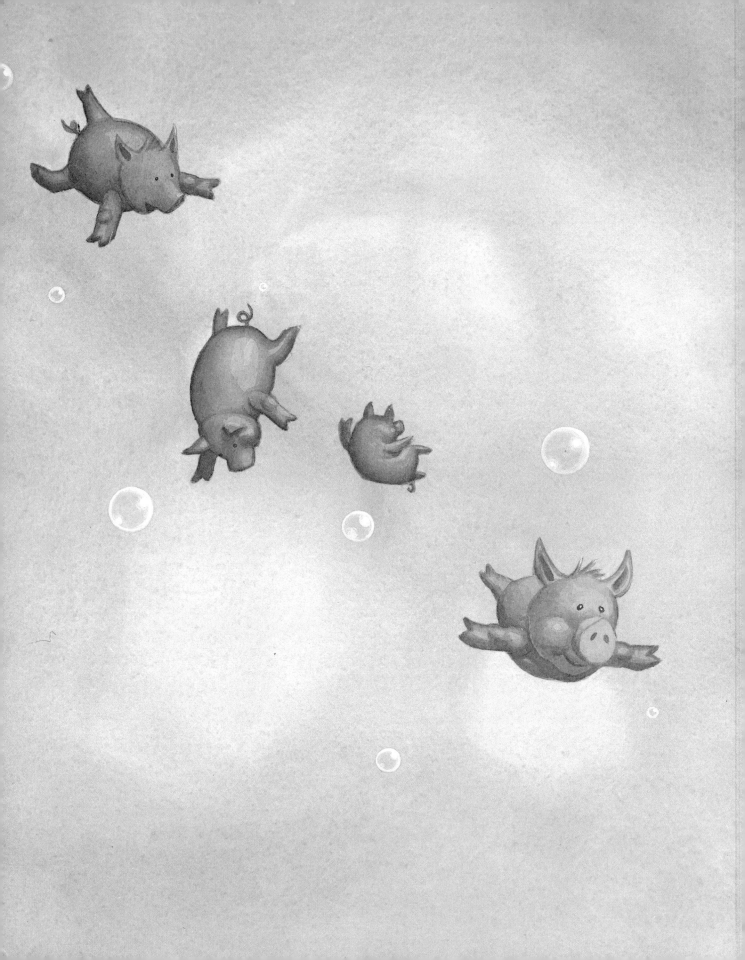